This book is
WANTED

and belongs to

. . . .

For
Francesca and Pui
Love D

For Laura,
who looks cute
when she wears a cowgirl suit
JE

First
published in
Great Britain 2006
This book and audio edition
published 2007 by Egmont UK Limited
239 Kensington High Street,
London W8 6SA

Text copyright © Jonathan Emmett 2006
Illustrations copyright © Deborah Allwright 2006
Music and lyrics copyright © Barry Gibson 2007
Recording copyright © Egmont UK Limited 2007

The author, illustrator and composer have asserted their moral rights

ISBN 978 1 4052 3042 1

1 3 5 7 9 10 8 6 4 2

A CIP catalogue record for this title is available from the British Library

Printed in Singapore

You can find out more about Jonathan Emmett's books
by visiting his website at www.scribblestreet.co.uk

She'll BE COMING Round the MOUNTAIN

Jonathan Emmett   Deborah Allwright

EGMONT

Gather round now!
I'm gonna tell y'all about a special visitor . . .

She'll be coming round the mountain
when she comes,

Toot-Toot!

She'll be coming round
the mountain when she comes,

Toot-Toot!

Yes, she'll whistle like a train,
As she speeds across the plain,
She'll be coming round the mountain
when she comes,

She'll be driving six white horses when she comes,

WHOA BACK!

She'll be driving six white horses when she comes,

WHOA BACK!

They're called Misty, Moonbeam, Milkshake,
Stardust, Silvermane and Snowflake,
She'll be driving six white horses
when she comes,

WHOA BACK!

Toot-Toot!

She'll be wearing
pink pyjamas when she comes,

Tee-Hee!

She'll be wearing pink pyjamas
when she comes,

Tee-Hee!

They are flowery and frilly,
And they make her look quite silly,
She'll be wearing pink pyjamas when she comes,

Tee-Hee!

WHOA BACK!

Toot-Toot!

She'll be juggling with jelly when she comes,

Squish-Splat!

She'll be juggling with jelly when she comes,

Squish-Splat!

If you ask her as a favour,
She will let you choose the flavour!
She'll be juggling with jelly when she comes,

Squish-Splat!

Tee-Hee!

WHOA BACK!

Toot-Toot!

And she'll dance across the rooftops when she comes,
Yee-Ha!
Yes, she'll dance across the rooftops when she comes,
Yee-Ha!

And you won't believe how nimbly
She can boogie round the **chimbly**,

Yes, she'll dance across the rooftops when she comes,

Yee-Ha!
Squish-Splat!
Tee-Hee!
WHOA BACK!
Toot-Toot!

DINER

JAIL

And she'll paint the whole town purple when she comes,

Bish-Bosh!

Yes, she'll paint the whole town purple when she comes,

Bish-Bosh!

And the place won't
look so glum,
When it's coloured
like a plum,

Yes, she'll paint the whole town purple when she comes,

And she'll drink out of a dustbin when she comes,

SLURP-SLURP!

Yes, she'll drink out of a dustbin when she comes,

SLURP-SLURP!

Unless it's ginger ale,
Which she drinks out of a pail,

Yes, she'll drink out of a dustbin when she comes,

And we'll all go out to meet her when she comes,

HI BABE!

Here she

And we'll all go out to meet her when she comes,

HI BABE!

So I hope that you are clear
On what to say when she gets here!

Because she's coming round the mountain . . .

comes!

Well I guess someone must have told y'all that I was comin'!

but this time doing these actions with each of the sounds?